The Susie K Files

S0-ABB-635

File name:
Life of the Party!

File No. #1

Shamini Flint

illustrated by
Sally Heinrich

ALLEN&UNWIN
SYDNEY·MELBOURNE·AUCKLAND·LONDON

For Erica, make me proud! SF
For M, science nerd *and* life of every party! SH

First published by Allen & Unwin in 2018

Allen & Unwin
83 Alexander Street
Crows Nest NSW 2065
Australia
Phone: (61 2) 8425 0100
Email: info@allenandunwin.com
Web: www.allenandunwin.com

A Cataloguing-in-Publication entry is available
from the National Library of Australia
www.trove.nla.gov.au

ISBN 978 1 76029 668 1

For teaching resources, explore
www.allenandunwin.com/resources/for-teachers

Cover design by Sandra Nobes
Text design by Sally Heinrich
Set in Gel Pen Upright Light by Sandra Nobes
This book was printed in November 2017 by McPherson's Printing Group, Australia.

10 9 8 7 6 5 4 3 2 1

My name is Susie K and I am a problem solver.

It is a good thing I am a
problem solver because,
even though I am
only nine years old,
I have a LOT of problems.
HUGE problems.
MEGA-HUGE PROBLEMS.

Problems as BIG as the Sydney Opera House...

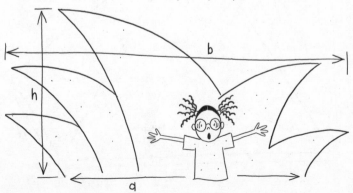

Problems as TALL as the Eiffel Tower...

Problems as MASSIVE as the pyramids of Egypt...

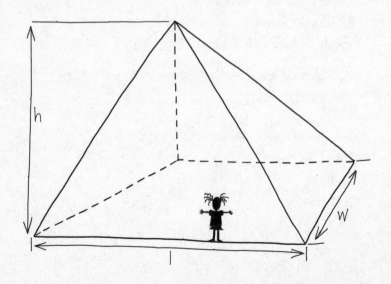

That's why I've decided to:

1. keep a FILE on each PROBLEM I have;
2. record my various EXPERIMENTS to solve the problem.

It is important to be organised if you are a problem solver.

Question
Hypothesis
Experiment
Result
Conclusion

Can you imagine what would happen if people didn't keep records?

What if the first person who ever found a dinosaur fossil didn't keep files?

What if Archimedes didn't write down what he discovered in the bath?

What if Orville and Wilbur Wright hadn't bothered to keep diagrams of their flying machines?

In fact, I have so many problems I'm not even sure which one to solve first!

PROBLEM NO. 1

I LOVE animals but...

I don't have a pet because I'm HIGHLY ALLERGIC to fur.

AH-CHOO!!!

AH-CHOO!

AH-CHOO!!

7

The closest thing I have to a pet is the class goldfish. He is also the only creature who listens to me when I speak.

I read somewhere that a goldfish's memory only lasts three seconds. So unless I repeat myself EVERY THREE SECONDS, George won't remember anything I've EVER said.

PROBLEM NO. 2

Problem No. 2 is MY FAMILY!!!! In fact, they're PROBLEM NO. 2, 3, 4... and 5 as well if you include the aunts!!!!!

First of all, there's Dad.

I think it is fair to say that Dad and I don't have a lot in common.

PROBLEM NO. 3

My brother Jack is not happy unless he's telling me that I'm rubbish at whatever I'm doing...

He also likes riddles.

Mind you, he has a point. I really am just RUBBISH at some of this stuff...

So why am I doing it?

That brings me to PROBLEM NO. 4!!!!

PROBLEM NO. 4

My mother wants me to be a HUGE success at everything I do. Music, sport, art, cooking, sewing... basically anything and everything.

She wants me to be a success at stuff that is FRANKLY IMPOSSIBLE!! Like wrestling crocs...

Or parachuting out of a plane...

Or heading for the stars...

And she doesn't just tell me WHAT to do...

She tells me WHEN to do it...

And HOW to do it!!! Even though she doesn't play the violin.

And if I complain?

Her solution to every problem is to tell me that she had much TOUGHER problems when she was young. This is probably true because my mum is Sri Lankan, and she arrived here as a refugee. (Sri Lanka is an island country near India.)

How do you argue with that?

Plus, she gave me the MOST RIDICULOUS name.

My full name is SUSANNA SAATHIAVANNI KANAGARATNAM-SMITH.

Susanna is the name of my dad's mother.

Mum consulted a Sri Lankan soothsayer who in turn consulted the stars and the planets and told my mum that I had to be called Saathiavanni or TERRIBLE THINGS would happen to me. What, pray tell, could be WORSE than being called Saathiavanni?

Sometimes, I stand outside on a beautiful starry night and shake my fist at the sky.

SMITH is my dad's surname and KANAGARATNAM
is my mother's surname.

Why aren't I just called
Susie Smith?

You guessed it...MUM!

You must have my father's name
because we had no male
relatives left after the war.

See what I mean? She did have it much tougher
than me...

Anyway, you can see why I need to solve some of these problems.

We have a report of an animal in distress in this house...

...most likely a cat?

GOAL!!

AAH CHOO!!

Hee hee hee hee!!!

Keep practising, Susie K!

I can't go through life as a girl with an unpronounceable name, an impossible family and a pet allergy!!!!

names

family

pet

21

The ONLY problem left was deciding which problem to solve first.

And then fate took a hand...

Mum walked me to school. (She doesn't usually but that morning she said she felt like a walk.)

When I was young, we never walked anywhere. We always had to run because of the danger...

We bumped into Sophie's mother and Sophie.

I knew what was coming next.

The fact of the matter is that I'm not exactly popular and I don't mind at all.

I prefer to be on my own because I like the people in books...

better than the people in real life...

I'm always chosen last as a PE partner because I REALLY, REALLY don't like sport.

And I used to get invited to parties but I never wanted to go because I'm not exactly the 'life of the party' sort...so I did my best to get out of them.

Now I don't get invited anymore which is a bit of a relief...

And I don't mind not having any close friends. After all, whenever I need someone to talk to I have George the Goldfish.

Also, the kids think I'm weird because I really, really like SCIENCE. I am going to be a scientist when I grow up and solve lots of problems...

including deforestation...

and endangered animals...

and plastic in the ocean.

Class lecture...

No one else in my class seems to like science that much.

Being the science teacher's pet doesn't help...

And also, there's that whole 'talking to a fish' thing...

I know I'll meet some kids one day who like animals and science and George as much as me and we'll be BEST FRIENDS FOREVER!!

But in the meantime, I've disappointed Mum.

And I REALLY, REALLY DON'T LIKE to disappoint Mum.

Partly, because she's my mum and I love her.

But mostly, because she's a problem solver just like me...except I never like her solutions.

I'm going to speak to your teachers about this party thing. It's not right that you're being left out and I want to know why it's happening.

NO!!!!

Parents only make problems at school WORSE. This is a well-known fact.

Like the time Joe's dad complained when he didn't make the track team.

So the coach put Joe in the track team.

Now the kids all call him 'Tortoise' but he has nowhere to retract his head like a real tortoise.

Or the time that Betty's mum did her art homework and then came in to complain when Betty didn't get an A.

Now the kids call her 'Picasso' even though she can't draw a stick figure (and her mum can't draw a cat).

Or the time that Ethan's parents said Ethan was acting up in class because he was too bright and was bored with the lessons...

The kids call him 'Einstein' now...

which is a bit of a waste of a joke because Mr Borderline Genius doesn't know who Einstein is!

Anyway, the point is that parents don't help in this sort of situation.

Unfortunately, I PANICKED.

So, I have no choice. The first HUGE problem that I have to solve is how to get invited to Clementine's party.

Why did it have to be CLEMENTINE? Even when I *was* being invited to parties, I probably wouldn't have been invited to hers...

She's the MOST POPULAR kid in school.

She's SO pretty...

She wears beautiful clothes (always in pink)...

She has the latest phone...

She comes to school in a convertible...

She IS the LIFE OF EVERY PARTY...

Well, I have no choice. I need to somehow get Clementine to invite me to her party or Mum will never get over it...

OPERATION 'LIFE OF THE PARTY'

I needed to talk to someone with friends. LOTS OF FRIENDS. I needed to talk to Jack.

Jack is four years older than me, so he's a teenager.

He is also VERY handsome. I know that because every time Mum's relatives come to visit, they tell him.

He's very POPULAR at school.

He's always got a gang of boys and girls with him.
They act as if everything he says is genius.

I asked him for advice.

He wasn't very helpful.

I decided to ask George...

I was stuck. I had NO IDEA how to get invited to the party. What sort of problem solver gets stuck so quickly??

Jack the Riddler was still no help...

Why does he think that's something to be proud of?

Let me think...

First, IDENTIFY the problem.

Second, ANALYSE the problem.

Third, IDENTIFY a solution.

Fourth, TEST the solution.

Fifth, REPEAT PROCESS ALL OVER AGAIN UNTIL SOLUTION FOUND.

And that's when it hit me!!!

The method to solve all problems, whatever they might be, is exactly the same!!

1. identify the problem
2. analyse the problem
3. find a solution
4. test the solution
5. repeat until THE PROBLEM IS SOLVED!!!

Easy peasy, lemon squeezy!!!

STEP 1: IDENTIFY THE PROBLEM
I need an invitation to Clementine's birthday party.

STEP 2: ANALYSE THE PROBLEM
I need to know when and where her party is being held, what sort of party it is, and which kids have been invited.

STEP 3: FIND A SOLUTION
Discover WHY they were invited to her party.

STEP 4: TEST THE SOLUTION
Do whatever it is that they did to get invited UNTIL . . .

STEP 5: THE PROBLEM IS SOLVED!!!
I get invited too!!!!

HERE WE GO!!!!

Three days later, I was ready.

Have you ever been chased around the school by a gang of angry girls?

Well, it's exactly like being chased by big dogs...

or lions...

or hostile aliens...

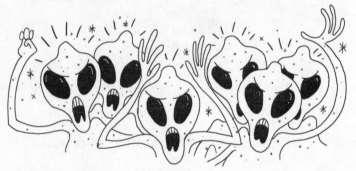

EXCEPT MUCH WORSE!!!

How do we solve the problem of being chased
by a big gang of angry kids?

Problem solved.

But I still haven't been invited to Clementine's party
and I'm running out of time...

The next day, I had a stroke of luck (sort of).

When I got to school, Clementine was sitting on a bench, sobbing her eyes out.

Great. So Clementine's mum (who works in advertising) only cares about the environment some of the time. Better than none of the time, I suppose.

And that's when I had my idea.

My extremely brilliant idea!!!

The BEST, most BRILLIANT IDEA in the WHOLE WORLD EVER!!!!!

Better than the invention of the automobile!

Better than the invention of the lightbulb!

I can see!

Is anybody there?

Hello?

Hello?

Hello?

Better than the invention of the telephone!

I waited till I could get Clementine alone.

60

First, we need to
examine a balloon.

* It is sort of ROUND.

* It is BRIGHTLY
  COLOURED.

I've got it.

Origami birds...

Back to the drawing board. And back to the balloon.

* It is sort of round.
* It is brightly coloured.
* It FLIES!!

Tomorrow is the day of the party. So if I don't find a solution to this balloon problem today, I'm TOAST.

I need something pink that flies that's not dangerous.

It has to be light...like this tissue paper.

I'm a problem-solving scientist! How hard can this be?

How do we get the tissue to float upwards instead of downwards?

Huff and puff?

Only possible for the big bad wolf,
not me.

THE EUREKA MOMENT

Back to the drawing board...and almost out of time.

EUREKA!!!!

This is what we do, George!!

By George, she's got it!

How come it's SO EASY for Mum to get invited to stuff?

Some of the other kids who liked the balloon substitutes came along early to help out too.

Susie K, where should we put these?

Put them along the driveway, please.

Susie K, where shall we hang the origami cranes and other animals?

How about here?

But we saved the BEST for last...

The kids all sat down for pizza.

I had put a single square piece of pink tissue paper and a pencil on each plate.

Clementine's mum and dad quickly lit the top of each tissue 'candle'.

Suddenly...

I guess some things don't change.

We had pizza...
birthday cake...

and played with the kites,
bubbles and pompoms...

Reading a book and messing with my chemistry set, with Bones to keep me company...

And George, of course!

Here's looking at you, kid.

File name:
THE SUSIE K FILES
LIFE OF THE PARTY!

File No. #1

CONFIDENTIAL

Case CLOSED!

But...